Silly Goose and Dizzy Duck Play Hide-and-Seek

Sally Grindley

Illustrated by Adrian Reynolds

Silly Goose and Dizzy Duck went for a walk in the woods. Suddenly, Silly Goose held onto Dizzy Duck's wing and said, "I think someone's following us."

They looked around,

but there was no one there.

"Silly me," said Silly Goose,

"I must be imagining things."

They walked on again.

Suddenly, Dizzy Duck leaped into the air and said,

"I heard a twig snap."

They turned slowly around and
saw Clever Fox tiptoeing away.

Cooeee!

"We can see you!" called Silly Goose.

"Are you playing hide-and-seek?"

"Can we play too?" said Dizzy Duck.

"All right," said Clever Fox.

He smiled a hungry smile.

"You hide while I count to five."

One!

Silly Goose tried to **squeeze** inside a hollow log . . .

but she was too **fat.**

Two!

Dizzy Duck

tried to climb

a tree . . .

but

he was scared

of heights.

Three!

Silly Goose crawled under a holly bush . . . **but**
it was
much too
prickly.

Four!
Dizzy Duck jumped into the river . . .

. . . but it was too cold.

Five!

Silly Goose scuttled under a pile of leaves.

Coming, ready or not!

Dizzy Duck squatted

behind a pile of stones.

"Which one shall I eat first?" sniggered Clever Fox.

"The silly goose or the dizzy duck?"

He began to look for them.

Dizzy Duck giggled.

Silly Goose sneezed.

Clever Fox crept up behind Dizzy Duck.

Grizzly Bear crept up behind Clever Fox.

BOOOOOOO! boomed Grizzly Bear.

Aaaaaaaah!

yelled Clever Fox and he shot
out of the woods.

"Just as well I came along when I did,"
chuckled Grizzly Bear.

"You frightened our friend,"
grumbled Silly Goose.

"And spoiled our game," said Dizzy Duck.

"You'll have to play instead."

One

Two

Three

Four

Five

Coming, ready or not!

called Silly Goose and Dizzy Duck.